STO

# Mr. Black's
# SECRET

*by*

## CATHRINE
# BARR

HENRY Z. WALCK, INC.    NEW YORK
1965

DEDICATED
WITH AFFECTION
TO MARIAN

U. S. 1321965

Mr. Black, the cat, peered around the corner.

On the porch a stranger was eating the food put there for Mr. Black by his family.

Mr. Black snarled! His back arched. Fur bristled! Tail twitched!

But surprise! After a friendly look, the stranger went on eating.

He was handsome , too,
with shining stripes on his
black coat.

Curious, Mr. Black circled
around, came closer.

The friendly stranger made
room for him and went on eating.

So, Mr. Black moved
cautiously in and
ate with him.

Thus Mr. Black and
Skunk became friends.

After that
Skunk came
quite often
to have supper
with Mr. Black.

Skunk usually rushed at the food. Sometimes his paw tipped the dish, spilling the supper. This annoyed Mr. Black who was very neat.

But Skunk was so friendly . . . . . Mr. Black overlooked his messiness.

After supper they played
together in the shadows until
Skunk left for the woods.

Sometimes Skunk gobbled the food so fast that Mr. Black hardly got any. But Mr. Black overlooked this rudeness.

One evening Skunk took
Mr. Black to see his den in the
woods.  They became better
friends than ever.

So Skunk came every evening
to have supper with Mr. Black.

Then one night the family put Mr. Black's food out early, while he was still snoozing upstairs.

While Mr. Black slept, Skunk came and ate the whole meal.

Later, when the family opened
the door for Mr. Black, they saw
the dish was empty.

"Who ate Mr. Black's food?" they
asked.

Mr. Black knew, but he just
looked away.

So the next night the family
watched secretly from the window.

Skunk came and
ate with Mr. Black.

The family was amazed to
see a skunk eating on the
porch with their pet.

At the window
they made not a
move. They didn't
want to startle
the skunk.

After Skunk had gone, they really fussed! They were alarmed! A skunk eating on their porch! He might spray his perfume on everything!

"We'll fix him!" father said. "We need a trap small enough, so he won't be able to spray."

The following night the family put out a box trap, with a dish of food inside for bait.

Mr. Black tried to warn his friend, but the hungry skunk dashed right into the trap after the food.

BANG went the
door behind him!

Skunk was a
prisoner!

Mr. Black looked for the
family. Luckily they were at
dinner and didn't hear the
commotion.

U. S. 1321965

The cat prowled
around the trap.
He peeked in. Skunk
ate, and peeked out.

Mr. Black sat. Could he
help his friend? He pawed at
the trap.

At last he got a claw under the
door and lifted it just a bit. Then
Skunk got his nose under it.

Finally, together, they lifted the door just enough for Skunk to wiggle out.

He looked at Mr. Black in his friendliest way, then ambled across the yard toward his den in the woods.

Mr. Black watched
from the porch, lick-
ing his paws.

The family came out.
They saw the closed trap
and seized it.   Nothing
inside  but the empty
dish!

No skunk!

They looked at Mr. Black
in wonderment.

"What happened?" they asked.

Mr. Black finished washing, smoothed his whiskers, and looked off over the hills.